Jamie and the Rola Polar Bear

Blackie Bears

LEABHARLANN CHONTAE MHUIGHEO

This book may be kept for two weeks. It may
be renewed if not required by another borrower.

The latest date entered is the date by which the
book should be returned.

Jamie and the Rola Polar Bear

Elisabeth Beresford

Illustrated by Janet Robertson

A Blackie Bear

For my foster children
For Ana – Ecuador, Bunhom – Thailand,
Samuel – Kenya, Kumara – India

S ∧ 36 879/5.

BLACKIE CHILDREN'S BOOKS

Published by the Penguin Group
Penguin Books Ltd, 27 Wrights Lane, London W8 5TZ, England
Penguin Books USA Inc., 375 Hudson Street, New York, New York 10014, USA
Penguin Books Australia Ltd, Ringwood, Victoria, Australia
Penguin Books Canada Ltd, 10 Alcorn Avenue, Toronto, Ontario, Canada M4V 3B2
Penguin Books (NZ) Ltd, 182–190 Wairau Road, Auckland 10, New Zealand

Penguin Books Ltd, Registered Offices: Harmondsworth, Middlesex, England

First published 1993
1 3 5 7 9 10 8 6 4 2
First edition

Text copyright © Elisabeth Beresford, 1993
Illustrations copyright © Janet Robertson, 1993

The moral right of the author and illustrator has been asserted

Set in 15/20 Monophoto Times New Roman Schoolbook

Printed and bound by Butler & Tanner Ltd, Frome and London

A CIP catalogue record for this book is available from the British Library

ISBN 0–216–94046–X

About the Author

Elisabeth Beresford is an established
children's author. This is her second
book for Blackie in the Blackie Bear
series, her first being *Tim the Trumpet*.
She has written over one hundred
books, including the enormously
popular Wombles series. She is a
freelance writer and journalist, and
has frequently broadcast on television
and radio. She has also spent time in
Africa, giving talks to children in
schools. Although she was born in
Paris, Elisabeth now lives on
Alderney, in the Channel Islands. In
between her writing she even finds
time to work as a Station Master on
the Alderney Railway!

'Mazing!' said Jamie.

It had started to snow in the
middle of the night, so when he
woke up and looked out of the
window the world had turned white.
It made everything look quite
different. Jamie lived on the top
floor of a very tall block of flats, so
it was rather like being on the

top of a mountain.

'Mazing,' said Jamie again, breathing on the window so that it misted over. The sun was quite pale, but it still made everything shimmer and glisten. Every bit of every roof was white. Far, far down below, the streets were white too, except for a few grey smudges where the traffic was trying to move. It wasn't moving much, though, and Jamie could just hear the angry growl it was making. He could also hear one of the lifts going down.

He pushed his nose right against the glass to try and see his mother leave the flats on her way to work. But there were too many heads and feet bobbing about and he couldn't make out which one was her.

'Bye, Mum,' said Jamie, breathing all over the glass and making it go misty. 'I'm going to get you a surprise today!'

The lift was starting to come up again. Jamie hated the lift. He didn't know why, he just did. And today he had to go in it on his own to get his mother's birthday present.

It was a Problem. He hadn't told anybody that he hated the lift in case he got teased about it. It made living on the top floor of Primrose Flats very awkward. He had to keep thinking of excuses to travel up and down with other people.

Usually he lurked in his front doorway until he saw one of the other flat doors open. Then he just sauntered out and joined whoever it was for the journey down. And he did the same thing when he had to come up, although the caretaker always gave him funny looks if he hung about too long. As though he was doing something wrong!

Jamie had another slice of bread and peanut butter while he thought things over. He looked out at the unfamiliar shining white world. He would have to go to the market soon. He sighed as he thought about going down in the lift. Then, as the window misted up again, he thought he saw something very strange and very exciting...

Jamie rubbed the window with his sleeve, held his breath and screwed up his eyes. There were a lot of heads and feet down there now, sliding and slipping. They were still moving faster than the traffic though, which seemed to have stuck. The yellow light by the black and white crossing (only it was all

12

white now) glowed like a setting sun. Standing right by it, looking left and right and left again, was a Polar Bear. There was no doubt about it. Jamie had only ever seen pictures of one before, but a Polar Bear is not an easy animal to mistake.

This one was very large and its fur looked a little grey and shabby against the snow. Jamie knew he was looking at a very lost Polar Bear. Nobody else seemed to be taking any notice of it, or trying to help.

Jamie knew it was up to him. The rest of the peanut butter vanished in a flash and he was into his boots, jacket and scarf in an instant. It's not every day you get the chance to

rescue a lost Polar Bear. He didn't hang about for anybody else outside the lift, but pushed the down button with an impatient finger. Jab, jab, jab. The lift slid up and yawned at him. Jamie fairly leapt inside.

He shifted from foot to foot as they whooshed downwards. Supposing the bear had vanished? Supposing somebody had taken it away? The lift seemed to take for ever.

Jamie shot out of the lift, across the hall and through the doors in world speed record time. It was a lot colder outside then he had realized. He felt his nose freeze up at once and his eyes watered.

He tried to run and he skidded, went sideways and found himself clinging to a bus stop. And there on the other side of the street was the bear, still looking very worried. His head was turning from side to side as though he didn't understand where he was or how to cross the road.

He saw Jamie on his side of the

road and gave a bearish sort of smile. It was rather like one friend recognizing another when they hadn't met for a long time. Jamie slipped and slid through the stuck traffic until they were standing face to face.

'I'm Jamie,' said Jamie.

'I'm Rola Polar Bear,' said Rola Polar Bear.

Rola Polar Bear had a deep husky voice and after a moment's hesitation he put out a large paw. Jamie shook it. They looked at each other. Nobody else took any notice at all. It was as if a seven-foot high Polar Bear wandered past every day of the week.

'I was wondering,' said Rola

Polar Bear.

'I wondered if...' said Jamie, both speaking together.

'You first,' said Rola Polar Bear, who was a polite sort of bear.

'It's my mum's birthday present. I don't know what to get. I thought somebody might come with me. You next.'

'I was looking for the North Pole. I seem to have lost it. But it won't run away so there's plenty of time. Very bright, your snow.' Rola Polar Bear unzipped a small pocket in his fur and took out a pair of dark glasses and put them on. 'Where will you get the present?'

'The Market,' said Jamie, starting to smile. Jamie usually looked

anxious. Now his frown was
melting away, rather like the snow
which was turning slushy on the
road.

Most days he didn't like the
Market much, but with a large
friend to talk to it might be fun.

'Mazing,' said Rola Polar Bear,
'we don't have many markets at the
North Pole. Which way do we go?'

Sliding and slipping they set off side by side, both of them talking at once as though they'd known each other for years. Nobody took any notice of them at all, except to skip out of the way every now and again.

But then most people wouldn't know a Rola Polar Bear if it came up and asked them the time.

'And it can't cost too much,' said Jamie as they turned into the Market, which, in spite of the snow, was already getting crowded.

You could buy anything in the Market. Clothes, furniture, books, food, and best of all toys. When Jamie was with his mother she would go off to the food part and

Jamie would plant himself in front
of the toys and just stare. A bicycle,
only one wheel, was a bargain at
only a pound. A lopsided football,
ninety pence. A rather scruffy
looking skateboard, two pounds.
Jamie knew them all by heart, but
today he had more serious things

on his mind. He made straight for a
certain stall, with Rola Polar Bear
following on behind.

'Mazing...' Rola Polar Bear said,
stooping down to stare at some bits
of wire and metal which could have
been the inside of anything.

'Please don't touch the merchan-
dise,' said the stall-holder without
looking up. But Jamie was already

pulling Rola Polar Bear away to a
stall right at the back of the
Market. It was covered in shawls.
Woollen, silk, patterned, plain,
thick, thin, as small as a handker-
chief or as big as a blanket. Jamie
beckoned Rola Polar Bear down to
his height so he could whisper in

one furry ear.

'Every time we come here Mum *always* stops and looks a lot, but she never buys anything. It's what she'd *really* like for her birthday. A shawl.'

Luckily this stall-holder didn't seem to mind them touching

anything. Quite soon Jamie had Rola Polar Bear standing with his arms spread out while Jamie hung shawls all over him. They looked a bit unusual, but the only person who took any notice was an old woman who stared at Rola Polar Bear very hard over the top of her spectacles. She sniffed and said something like, 'I suppose it's the weather...' and moved on.

Jamie found it very difficult to make up his mind. He would have hated shopping on his own, but it was quite fun with Rola Polar Bear.

A group of bigger boys came sliding through the Market throwing rather dirty snowballs.

Jamie ducked, expecting one of

them to hit him. Rola Polar Bear
scooped up two big pawfuls of
snow, patted them into an
enormous ball and lobbed it over
the stall. It was like a small
avalanche and the boys went
skidding off as fast as they could.

'I enjoy a good snow fight,' said
Rola Polar Bear. He sighed gently

as he thought of his lost home at the North Pole. He dusted down his paws and took two lollies out of his zip pocket.

'Thanks,' said Jamie. He pointed to the shawl draped over Rola Polar Bear's left arm. 'That's definitely the one Mum would like. The one with the butterflies and things. Hope it doesn't cost too much...'

'How much have you got?' asked the stall-holder, stamping his feet and blowing on his hands. The sky had turned a nasty yellow colour and it was getting colder by the minute. People's noses were turning pink and their eyes were watering. The only happy face belonged to

Rola Polar Bear as he sniffed the
air. 'Straight off the ice-cap,' he
muttered to himself.

'Three pounds,' said Jamie,
emptying out the old sweet packet
where he kept his money.

'Three pounds it is then,' said the
stall-holder, beginning to gather up
all the shawls as the first snowflakes
started to drift down. 'That's a

bargain you've got there, belonged
to an Indian princess I dare say.
Here's something to wrap it up in.
Pity to get snow on it.'

'I'll carry it,' said Rola Polar Bear.

'You're big enough to carry the
stall, you are,' said the stall-holder.
'With all that fur I don't suppose
you feel the cold much?'

'Not much,' agreed Rola Polar
Bear.

He and Jamie wandered around
for a bit. The gang of boys came
back into the Market, but they kept
well away and Jamie grinned to
himself. Nobody was going to make
any trouble when Rola Polar Bear
was around. Jamie decided that the
next stop should be the playground.

The snow was turning into a white mist by now and there was nobody else about. Rola Polar Bear took one look at the slide, handed the shawl over to Jamie and rushed towards it. He went down on his front, on his back, standing up, and finally on one paw. He was very good at it.

At last, quite out of breath and covered in snow from head to paw, he rejoined Jamie. 'I get a bit of practice on the snow slopes,' he said. He shook himself violently.

Suddenly Jamie's happiness wavered.

'Do you want to go home *now*?' he asked sadly.

'Oh no, not just yet. To be honest

this is mazingly like home, only there's more to do here.'

Jamie felt happier and suddenly discovered that he was very hungry indeed. They slipped and slithered their way back, both of them talking and neither of them listening, until they reached the flats.

It was as if they had been friends for years.

The caretaker came out of his office and gave them one of his suspicious looks, but Jamie only smiled and walked – well, slithered – over to the lifts and pressed a button as though he'd been bossing lifts about all his life.

'My word!' said Rola Polar Bear, looking at all the buttons and

knobs. 'How do you manage to
work one of these things?'

'There's nothing to it really,' said
Jamie, pressing one button after
another. As Rola Polar Bear had
never been in a lift before he kept
very quiet, and he seemed quite
glad to get out when they reached
the top floor.

'You soon get used to it,' said Jamie.

His mother had left some food to be heated up in the stove. There was a message on the answer-phone asking Jamie to ring her at work when he got back.

'She's got to work an extra shift,' explained Jamie, as he put the phone down. But Rola Polar Bear wasn't listening to Jamie. He was peering suspiciously at the fish and chips.

'Would you mind,' he said, 'if I have mine without the cooking?' And he unzipped his pocket and took out a packet (extra large) of fish fingers.

As it grew dark Jamie started to

worry again.

'Will you want to go home *now*?' he asked again sadly.

'Well, I was wondering,' said Rola Polar Bear, 'as we're having such a good time, if I could sort of stay round here. Somewhere. Just for a bit...'

They looked at each other. Rola Polar Bear took two choc-ices out of his zip pocket and handed one over. Jamie thought very hard. He wasn't too sure what his mother would say if she came home to find a very large Polar Bear in their small flat. Especially after a double shift. And then he had the most terrific idea.

'I tell you what,' said Jamie, 'there's this shed place up on the roof. It's something to do with the lifts, I think. The caretaker took Mum and me up there once. It's got a sink and bunks and a table, and you can see for miles and miles. When it's not snowing.'

'Just what I wanted,' said Rola Polar Bear. 'Now shall we wrap up that shawl all ready for tomorrow

and then perhaps we can have
another bit of supper.'

The shawl was not easy to wrap
up neatly, and it kept sliding about.

In the end Rola Polar Bear stood
on one edge of the paper and
together they managed somehow.

Rola Polar Bear produced
another snack, which they ate

hungrily.

Soon both of them were yawning. Jamie showed Rola Polar Bear up to the roof and pointed out the shed.

'Mazing,' said Rola Polar Bear. 'Just like home. See you tomorrow then.' Jamie watched Rola Polar Bear as he set off through the snow, leaving enormous paw prints behind him which were soon covered up.

Rola Polar Bear settled down in the shed, rubbed the window with his paw and took a pair of binoculars out of his zip pocket.

He was almost sure he could see the Northern Lights. He sighed a little and then Jamie saw his head nod slowly forwards. 'Good night

43

Rola Polar Bear,' he whispered.
'See you tomorrow.'

Jamie woke up with a tremendous
start, his heart racing. For a moment
he couldn't remember where he was
or why he was suddenly so worried.
Then he remembered Rola Polar
Bear and the wonderful day they'd
had together.

Or had they? Had he just made it
all up? Was there really a Rola
Polar Bear with a zip pocket in his
fur? In the middle of the night it all
seemed like a dream.

Jamie began to worry and worry
and worry. He crawled out of bed
and felt his way over to the
window. It was snowing more than

ever. Even by pressing his nose
right up against the glass he
couldn't see the hut on the roof.
That too had vanished.

Jamie got down on his knees and
craned his head right round.
Nothing. Except that his knees were
getting cold and damp.

DAMP!

Jamie jumped to his feet and held
the curtain right up. By the
yellowish light of the street lamps

he could see them quite clearly.

TWO LARGE SOGGY PAWMARKS. That was where Rola Polar Bear had stood while they struggled to wrap up the shawl. Rola Polar Bear was real all right and at this moment was probably snoring up on the roof!

Tomorrow there would be a hundred wonderful things they could do. Like getting Rola Polar Bear and his mother to meet for a start? At least with his magic pocket she wouldn't have to worry about feeding him. In fact here were no worries at all!

'Mazing! *Mazing!* MAZING!' said Jamie, and did a backflip on to and into his bed. And in less than a minute he was fast asleep, to make tomorrow arrive as fast as possible.

Mazing.